Sammy the Hippo

COLLINGWOOD O'HARE ENTERTAINMENT LTD
Created by Trevor Ricketts and Christopher O'Hare
Series developed by Tony Collingwood
Copyright © 2001 by Collingwood O'Hare Entertainment Ltd.

First published in Great Britain in 2001 by HarperCollins*Children's Books*,
a division of HarperCollins*Publishers* Ltd,
77-85 Fulham Palace Road, Hammersmith, London W6 8JB.
ISBN: 0 00 710876 1
1 3 5 7 9 10 8 6 4 2
A CIP catalogue record for this title is available from the British Library.

The HarperCollins website address is:
www.**fire**and**water**.com

Printed and bound in Hong Kong

ANIMAL
STORIES

Sammy the Hippo

Written by Lucy Daniel-Raby

Collins

An imprint of HarperCollins*Publishers*

Sammy the Hippo
Loved his mud pool.
He liked getting mucky –
He thought mud was cool.

He'd dive in from high,
His feet over his head,
And make a big splash,
Which his Mum learnt to dread.

He'd rub mud and smear it
Between all his toes.
It's amazing the places
A Hippo's mud goes.

What he liked best
Was to stick his head under,
And make a rude noise
With bubbles, like thunder.

His Mummy would watch him;
She wasn't so keen,
For she liked to keep things
All tidy and clean.

Her house was so pretty –
All flowers and lace.
She dusted and polished,
And kept things in their place.

Well, can you imagine
Her utter dismay,
At the dreadful result
Of his muddy display?

He'd left dirty footprints
On her shiny clean floor.
And big Hippo hand prints
On the walls and the door.

His Mummy got cross
And made her thoughts clear.
"You must never, not ever,
Bring mud into here!"

Poor Sammy was sorry,
But what could he do?
He loved mud so much –
But he loved his Mum too.

After a bath,
Sam sat on Mum's knee.
"Please try," said his Mum,
"To stay clean like me."

She gave him a hug,
And Sam said he'd try –
Even though mud was best –
He'd try to stay dry.

In the post next morning
Came an invite to play,
From Molly the Monkey
At her house the next day.

Her birthday party
Was the talk of the town.
There'd be bouncy castles
And a pantomime clown.

"Oh please can I go?"
Said Sammy excited.
His Mummy said, "Yes!
We've both been invited."

"Hooray!" cried out Sam.
"What shall I wear?"
He chose his red shoes,
And Mum combed his hair.

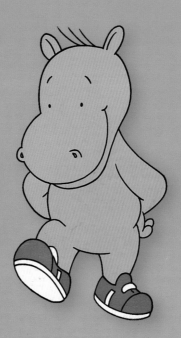

And what a great party
It turned out to be.
Molly's garden was full –
There was so much to see.

They both had such fun
And, to Sammy's surprise,
He came first in the sack race
And was awarded a prize.

Then all of the grown-ups
Where allowed just one race.
And Sammy cheered loudly
As his Mum made first place.

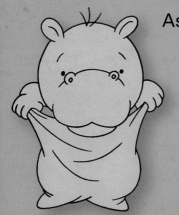

So they both won a present –
Sam's was a Gnome!
But Mum kept hers wrapped
Until they got home.

They sat by the pool –
Sam sat on Mum's knee.
Mum unwrapped her present.
What could it be?

Well, the prize that she'd got
For winning her race,
Was some kind of make-up
To put on her face.

A quick-drying mud pack
Called "Beauty Sublime",
That would give her smooth skin
In next to no time.

They both fell back laughing.
Mud for his Mummy!
Then Sam laughed again –
It was ever so funny.

Mum was delighted
And had to agree,
"Perhaps mud is good
For you AND for me!"

Now they both enjoy mud,
For beauty and play,
But both wash it off
At the end of the day!

The End